PETAL AND POPPY

AND THE PENGUIN

For information about permission to reproduce selections from this
book, write to Permissions, Houghton Mifflin Harcourt Publishing
Company, 215 Park Avenue South, New York, New York 10003.

www.hmhbooks.com

The text of this book is set in Cheltenham.
The display type was hand-lettered.
The illustrations were created digitally.

The Library of Congress Cataloging-in-Publication Data
Jahn-Clough, Lisa.
Petal and Poppy and the penguin / by Lisa Clough and Ed Briant.
p. cm.
Summary: Best friends Petal, the tuba-playing elephant, and Poppy,
the adventurous rhinoceros, have very different reactions when
they discover a penguin in their garden one stormy day.
ISBN 978-0-544-13330-3 paperback
ISBN 978-0-544-13770-7 paper over board
[1. Best friends—Fiction. 2. Friendship—Fiction. 3. Elephants—
Fiction. 4. Rhinoceroses—Fiction. 5. Penguins—Fiction.] I. Briant,
Ed, illustrator. II. Title.
PZ7.J153536Pfp 2014
[E]—dc23
2013020668

Manufactured in China
SCP 10 9 8 7 6 5 4 3 2 1

4500451496

PETAL

AND

POPPY

AND THE PENGUIN

BY LISA CLOUGH AND ED BRIANT

HOUGHTON MIFFLIN HARCOURT
Boston New York

11

31